Five Little Monkeys Sitting in a Tree

EILEEN CHRISTELOW

CLARION BOOKS

NEW YORK

For a new batch of little monkeys—
Gregory, Sebastian, Nicole, Julia, and Olivia.

Clarion Books
a Houghton Mifflin Company imprint
215 Park Avenue South, New York, NY 10003
Text and illustrations copyright © 1991
by Eileen Christelow

Printed in the U.S.A.

Library of Congress Cataloging-in-Publication Data
Christelow, Eileen.
Five little monkeys sitting in a tree / written and illustrated by Eileen Christelow.
p.   cm.
Summary: Five little monkeys sitting in a tree discover, one by one, that it is unwise
to tease Mr. Crocodile.
ISBN 0-395-54434-3   PA ISBN 0-395-66413-6
[1. Monkeys—Fiction. 2. Crocodile—Fiction. 3. Counting. 4. Stories in rhyme] I. Title.
PZ8.3.C456Fk 1991
[E]—dc20   90-40008
CIP   AC

WOZ   25 24 23 22 21

Five little monkeys and their mama
walk down to the river for a picnic supper.

Mama spreads out a blanket
and settles down for a snooze . . .

. . . while five little monkeys
climb a tree to watch Mr. Crocodile.

Five little monkeys, sitting in a tree,
tease Mr. Crocodile, "Can't catch me!"

Along comes Mr. Crocodile . . .

Oh, no! Where is she?

Four little monkeys, sitting in a tree,
tease Mr. Crocodile, "Can't catch me!"
Along comes Mr. Crocodile . . .

SNAP!

13

Oh, no! Where is he?

Three little monkeys, sitting in a tree,
tease Mr. Crocodile, "Can't catch me!"
Along comes Mr. Crocodile . . .

15

Oh, no! Where is he?

Two little monkeys, sitting in a tree,
tease Mr. Crocodile, "Can't catch me!"
Along comes Mr. Crocodile . . .

Oh, no! Where is she?

Now there's only one little
monkey, sitting in the tree,
teasing Mr. Crocodile,
"Can't catch me!"
Along comes Mr. Crocodile . . .

SNAP!

Oh, no! There are no little monkeys sitting in the tree. But, wait! Look!

1 2 3 4 5

Five little monkeys, sitting in the tree!

Their mama hugs them.

Their mama scolds them.
"Never tease a crocodile.
It's not nice—and it's dangerous."

Then five little monkeys and their mama
eat a delicious picnic supper.

And they do not tease Mr. Crocodile again!